Franklin and the Big Kid

From an episode of the animated TV series *Franklin*
produced by Nelvana Limited, Neurones France s.a.r.l.
and Neurones Luxembourg S.A., based on the Franklin
books by Paulette Bourgeois and Brenda Clark.

TV tie-in adaptation written by Sharon Jennings and
illustrated by Sean Jeffrey, Jelena Sisic and Shelley Southern.

Based on the TV episode *Franklin Delivers*, written by
John van Bruggen.

Franklin is a trademark of Kids Can Press Ltd.
The character Franklin was created by Paulette Bourgeois and Brenda Clark.
Text © 2002 Context*x* Inc.
Illustrations © 2002 Brenda Clark Illustrator Inc.

Kids Can Press acknowledges the financial support of the Ontario Arts Council,
the Canada Council for the Arts and the Government of Canada, through
the BPIDP, for our publishing activity.

Published in Canada by   Published in the U.S. by
Kids Can Press Ltd.   Kids Can Press Ltd.
29 Birch Avenue   2250 Military Road
Toronto, ON M4V 1E2   Tonawanda, NY 14150

www.kidscanpress.com

Edited by Tara Walker and Jennifer Stokes

Printed in Hong Kong, China, by Wing King Tong Company Limited

CM 02 0 9 8 7 6 5 4 3 2 1

National Library of Canada Cataloguing in Publication Data

Jennings, Sharon
    Franklin and the big kid

(A Franklin TV storybook)
The character Franklin was created by Paulette Bourgeois and Brenda Clark.

ISBN 1-55337-054-6

I. Jeffrey, Sean II. Sisic, Jelena III. Southern, Shelley IV. Bourgeois, Paulette
V. Clark, Brenda VI. Title. VII. Series: Franklin TV storybook.

PS8569.E563F715 2002   jC813'.54   C2002-900709-7

PZ7J429877Fr 2002

Kids Can Press is a *Corus*™ Entertainment company

Franklin and the Big Kid

Kids Can Press

FRANKLIN could count by twos and tie his shoes. He could slip and slide down the riverbank and swing all the way across the monkey bars. But some days, Franklin wished he could do more. Some days, Franklin wished he could do the things the big kids did.

One morning, Franklin looked at himself in the mirror.

"Have I grown since yesterday?" he asked his mother.

"Maybe just a little bit," she replied.

Franklin smiled and put on his cap.

"Your cap is on backwards," his mother said.

"I know," said Franklin. "This is how Jack Rabbit wears his cap. All the big kids do."

Franklin met Bear at the tree house to play pirates.

"Someone's coming, captain," whispered Franklin as he peered through the telescope.

"Friend or foe, matey?" asked Bear.

Franklin looked again.

"It's Jack Rabbit!" he exclaimed.

Franklin scrambled down to the ground.

"Hi, Jack," said Franklin. "What are you doing?"

"Just hanging around," replied Jack. "What are you doing?"

"I'm just hanging around, too," Franklin answered.

"If you want, you can come to the park later and watch me skateboard," said Jack.

"Wow! Thanks!" said Franklin.

Franklin said goodbye to Bear and hurried home for lunch.

"I'm meeting Jack Rabbit at the park," he told his parents.

He pulled on a soccer jersey.

"Are you playing a game?" asked his father.

Franklin shook his head.

"Jack always wears a jersey. And I want to be just like Jack."

Franklin rode his bike to the park. All afternoon he watched Jack and his friends do tricks on their skateboards.

"Want to try, Franklin?" asked Jack.

"Sure!" exclaimed Franklin. He stepped eagerly onto the board. He pushed off and stayed on for ten whole seconds.

"Wow!" said Jack. "You're almost as good as me."

Franklin grinned.

That night, Franklin asked his parents for
a skateboard.

"You just got a new bike," said his father.

"Bikes are for little kids," replied Franklin.

"Skateboards are dangerous," his mother
pointed out.

"But I'm good at skateboarding," answered
Franklin. "Jack said so."

"Maybe when you're bigger," said his father.

"I'm big enough," muttered Franklin.

The next morning, Bear called on Franklin.
"Do you want to play pirates?" he asked.
"Not today," Franklin replied. "I'm going to hang around with Jack. Do you want to come?"
"No thanks," Bear answered. "I'd rather play pirates."

After Bear left, Franklin hurried over to Jack's house.

"Do you want to skateboard?" Franklin asked.

"I can't," answered Jack. "I have to do my paper route."

Franklin offered to help.

"It isn't easy," said Jack. "I've got lots of papers to deliver and loads of flyers."

"I don't mind," Franklin replied. "I'm not a little kid, you know."

It took two hours for Jack and Franklin to sort the papers and insert all the flyers.

"This is a lot of work," said Franklin.

"It sure is," agreed Jack. "But I make lots of money."

That gave Franklin an idea. Maybe he could get his own paper route and buy a skateboard!

Franklin and Jack took turns lugging the wagon along the streets and tossing the papers at everyone's door. They had to go back to Jack's house four times to load up.

On the second trip, Franklin's tummy began to growl.

"Can we get something to eat?" he asked.

Jack shook his head. "I have to deliver everything by one o'clock," he replied.

On the third trip, the wind started to blow. Franklin ran after fly-away papers.

On the fourth trip, it started to rain. Franklin got soaked.

"It's a good thing you make lots of money," he said to Jack. "Think of all the neat stuff you can buy!"

But Jack explained that he was saving most of his money for college.

Franklin was grumpy and wet, tired and hungry when all the papers were finally delivered. Then he had an idea and cheered up.

"Do you want to skateboard?" he asked.

"Sorry, Franklin," said Jack. "I've got school work to do."

Jack thanked Franklin and gave him two dollars for helping.

"Thanks, Jack. See you later," called Franklin.

On the way home, Franklin thought about his two dollars. He thought about how many papers he would have to deliver before he could buy a skateboard.

Then, as Franklin passed the candy store, he thought a little more.

"Maybe I'm not big enough for a paper route and a skateboard," he decided.

After lunch, Franklin ran to the tree house.
"I've brought treasure, captain!" he called to Bear.
He held up a bag full of candy.
"Permission to come aboard," Bear answered.
And Franklin turned his cap the right way around
and climbed into the pirate ship.